Date: 10/20/16

FIGMENT

JOURNEY INTO IMAGINATION, VOLUME 4

Spotlight   Disney KINGDOMS   MARVEL

ABDOPUBLISHING.COM

Reinforced library bound edition published in 2016 by Spotlight,
a division of ABDO, PO Box 398166, Minneapolis, Minnesota 55439.
Spotlight produces high-quality reinforced library bound editions for
schools and libraries. Published by agreement with Marvel Characters, Inc.

Printed in the United States of America, North Mankato, Minnesota.
092015
012016

THIS BOOK CONTAINS
RECYCLED MATERIALS

marvelkids.com
© 2016 MARVEL

Elements based on Figment © Disney.

CATALOGING-IN-PUBLICATION DATA

Zub, Jim.
 Figment : journey into imagination / writer, Jim Zub ; artist, Filipe Andrade
and John Tyler Christopher. -- Reinforced library bound edition.
  p. cm. (Figment : journey into imagination)
"Marvel."
Summary: Dive into a steampunk fantasy story exploring the never-before-
revealed origin of the inventor known as Dreamfinder, and how one little
spark of inspiration created a dragon called Figment.
ISBN 978-1-61479-445-5 (vol. 1) -- ISBN 978-1-61479-446-2 (vol. 2) -- ISBN
978-1-61479-447-9 (vol. 3) -- ISBN 978-1-61479-448-6 (vol. 4) -- ISBN 978-1-
61479-449-3 (vol. 5)
1. Figment (Fictitious character)--Juvenile fiction. 2. Dragons--Juvenile
fiction. 3. Adventure and adventures--Juvenile fiction. 4. Graphic novels-
-Juvenile fiction. I. Andrade, Filipe, illustrator. II. Christopher, John Tyler,
illustrator. III. Title.
741.5--dc23

2015955126

Spotlight

A Division of ABDO
abdopublishing.com

...reality is a bit more *difficult*.

My *Mesmonic Spark Converter* brought us to a strange dimension of *dreams*...and now we've found the *nightmares* that come along with it.

Journey Into Imagination
Part Four

JIM ZUB writer
FILIPE ANDRADE artist
JEAN-FRANCOIS BEAULIEU colorist
VC'S JOE CARAMAGNA letterer

JOHN TYLER CHRISTOPHER cover artist

JIM CLARK, BRIAN CROSBY,
ANDY DIGENOVA, TOM MORRIS
& JOSH SHIPLEY
walt disney imagineers

MARK BASSO assistant editor
BILL ROSEMANN editor

AXEL ALONSO editor in chief
JOE QUESADA chief creative officer
DAN BUCKLEY publisher

special thanks to
DAVID GABRIEL

H!

FIGMENT

Blarion Mercurial, a young inventor at the **Academy Scientifica-Lucidus,** has been having a strange week. His assignment to develop an alternate energy source resulted in the **Integrated Mesmonic Converter.** The device blew up on its first run, then brought his childhood friend to life—a dragon called, appropriately enough, **Figment**—before pulling Blair and Figment into a dream-like world.

Chairman Illocrant, Blair's boss, wasn't thrilled with these results, and in attempting to shut down the chaotic machine inadvertently opened a doorway to another realm called **Clockwork Control,** allowing its leader, the **Singular,** to come to Earth. To begin his world domination by putting England "in order," the Singular summoned the first wave of his **Clockwork Army** through the portal.

While exploring their new surroundings, Blair and Figment met a metal-hungry but friendly winged creature called **Chimera,** who fled when they encountered the not-so-friendly **Sound Sprites.** They promptly captured the pair and shoved them in the "bass-ment" dungeon deep within the Audio Archipelago.

There they met **Fye,** a Sound Sprite jailed for his inability to "sound" properly. While captive, Figment triggered a realization for Blair—that the whole dream world sprang from his imagination and could be affected by his thoughts. Blair imagined a key for their cell, and wings to escape (which arrived in the form of Chimera to the rescue). The Sound Sprites gave chase, leading the group into the **NIGHTMARE NATION.**

That can't be as bad as it sounds, right?

ABANDONED!

NO! You pulled us apart!

HOPELESS!

There's *always* hope!

YOU'RE NOT EVEN REAL!

That... that's not *true*. I'm real as long as Blair believes in me!

HE DOESN'T BELIEVE IN ANYTHING ANYMORE.

Oh... That's not good.

POP

© Disney

**Early Figment and Dreamfinder character designs
for the Journey Into Imagination ride by X Atencio**

Artwork courtesy of Walt Disney Imagineering Art Collection